me! (JUST LiKE YOU,
ONLY BETTER)

Think you can handle *another* Jamie Kelly diary?

AND DON'T MISS JAMIE'S NEXT DIARY!

Jim Benton's Tales from Mackerel Middle School

DEAR DUMB DIARY,

ME! (JUST LIKE YOU, ONLY BETTER)

BY JAMIE KELLY

SCHOLASTIC INC.

New York   Toronto   London   Auckland
Sydney   Mexico City   New Delhi   Hong Kong

ISBN 978-0-545-11616-9

12 11 10 9 8 7 6 5 4 3 2 1   11 12 13 14 15 16/0

Printed in the U.S.A.   40

First printing, June 2011

For Griffin, Summer, and Mary K

*Thanks to Kristen LeClerc and to the
team at Scholastic: Shannon Penney,
Steve Scott, Elizabeth Krych, Susan Jeffers,
and Anna Bloom. You all make me just
like me, only better.*

THiS DiARY

property of

Jamie Kelly

SPECIAL TALENT - MUSIC CHOOSING, ART, ALL OTHER KNOWN TALENTS

LIKES - MUSIC, MYSELF, ME

DISLIKES - COPYCATS UNLESS THEY ARE REAL CATS.

I KNOW YOU'RE JUST
trying to figure
out how to
be like me...
well, here's A TIP...

THERE'S NOTHING I LIKE BETTER THAN NOT READING SOMEBODY'S DIARY.

ALSO, If I ever thought about doing it, I'd get her a REALLY GREAT present for her Birthday which is coming up....

Dear Whoever Is Reading My Dumb Diary,

Stop it.

I know you're hoping to read my diary and find out what it is about me that makes me so awesome.

And you probably want to steal my beauty secrets, like how not trying to be beautiful all the time makes me beautifuller. Or how I always discover the best bands before anybody else does.

Or maybe you're hoping to get a glimpse of my **supersecret** art secrets, like how I make glitter stick to things. (Okay, maybe that one is not that secret, but I do have other things about me that are way greater than they need to be.)

"Way Greater Than She Needs To Be." I'm getting older now, and I need to think about the future. So I officially authorize that saying to be engraved on the first twenty large statues people create of

me. After that, they can choose other super-complimentary things.

Frequent use of the word "cute" is also authorized, although I really prefer "kewt." (It's kewter.)

Also, parents, if you're reading this, stop reading my diary **now**. I know I'm not supposed to point out other people's flaws, but I didn't actually point them out, I only **wrote** them out. And if you punish me for it, I'll know that you read my diary. Not only am I not giving you permission to do that, it will just prove how much less awesome you are than me.

Signed, *Jamie Kelly*

P.S. If you are a really great **world-famous** band, you are allowed to read my diary and make songs about the most beautiful parts. But in fairness, I can't permit anybody but me to hear them.

Sunday 01

Dear Dumb Diary,

One year I asked for a puppy for my birthday, but my dad got me a pogo stick instead. I went out to the driveway to try it out, but I fell and broke my wrist.

When we got back from the emergency room, my dad felt so bad that he went out and **bought me a puppy**.

LAUNCH

FLIGHT

FREEFALL

BOING

IMPACT

I was so happy that I threw my arms wide open to give the puppy a hug and accidentally hit my dad in the face with my cast and **broke his nose.**

When he got back from the emergency room, I tried to make him feel better by being outside in the driveway playing with the pogo stick, but I was even clumsier with my cast on and I lost control of it again. At least that time I didn't fall and break anything.

But I did put a **six-inch scratch** in his new car.

Soon the puppy decayed into the lumpy, toadish bucket of unpleasantness we know as Stinker, who recently fathered a smaller version of his stinky self we know as Stinkette. The pogo stick remains unused in the garage and we never see it anymore, except for the five times it has gone unsold at garage sales. Dad never got the scratch fixed, and his nose still makes an awful noise when he snores.

The moral of this birthday story is this: Getting what you ask for can be the **worst thing** that ever happened to you. Also, not getting it can be the worst.

FRESH, QUIET AIR IN

SOUNDS OF BEAR BEING MUTILATED BY BULLDOZER OUT

The reason I bring up this tragic story is that my birthday is coming up soon, and this one is going to be very different from **"Broken-arm Birthday."** (Or, as it is also known, "Swear-swear-swear-nose-swear Birthday.")

It's going to be the best birthday ever because I'm only asking for music, and I'm pretty sure Dad won't try to swap in a pogo stick or any of the other dangerous substitutions he's attempted over the years. My guess: gift certificate.

Plus, this year I was prepared. My parents are old and therefore only like music that was recorded before people got good at it, but I made it very clear that I want **MY** favorite music and not theirs.

One of the Rock Bands my parents listened to

Also — **BONUS!** — they said I can have a party, and figuring out who you want to invite and exclude is super-fun.

Birthdays Past

WHAT I ASKED FOR	WHAT I RECEIVED
A koala Bear	A teddy Bear
A Narwhal	A sardine with a toothpick in its head (thanks, Isabella)
Six-inch heels	A Lecture from Dad

Monday 02

Dear Dumb Diary,

Art class today!

My art teacher, as you may recall, Dumb Diary, is Miss Anderson, who is so beautiful and gorgeous and ravishing that women have a strong natural impulse to push her in front of a train. (Wouldn't it be **great** to be admired like that?)

Today she gave us a new assignment: to make a **MUSIC POSTER!!!!!!!!!!** I am seriously excited enough to do way more exclamation points than that, but I want to tell you about the assignment and not waste any more time on **punctuational extremism.**

Miss Anderson handed out the thin sheets of poster board that we'll be using to portray our favorite band or performer or whatever. Then she went around the room and we all named who we were going to draw.

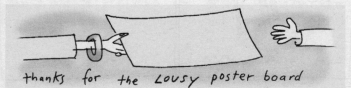

thanks for the LOUSY poster board

I'm going to do a poster for this one band that's so cool that its name **can't even be spelled.**

It's pronounced like if you take a big inhale of air and then let it all out of your mouth at once, really low, like you're kind of frustrated and tired and a little disgusted.

I feel like I have a real connection to this band because I was making this sound long before I ever heard of them. This sound can also be made by stepping on the bloated abdomen of a sleeping beagle, accidentally or on purpose.

Since their name can't be spelled, they go by the name **FATAALD**, which you get by using the first letters in Frustrated And Tired And A Little Disgusted.

Ladies and Gentlemen — FATAALD

FATAALD is really popular. They've sold, like, a **kajillion** albums or something, and my dad hates them, which is always a great way to tell if a band is good. (You can use this method, in fact, to tell if **many** things are good.)

Stuff My Dad Hates

NAIL DEVOTION

BEAUTIFUL MUSICAL LOUDNESS

ALL KNOWN WONDERFULNESS

MOVEMENT

Since I was the **first person** I know of that liked them, that means that I own them a little, and anybody at my school who listens to them is copying me and trespassing. I'm not making this up. This is **AN ACTUAL LAW** that you could **ACTUALLY GET ARRESTED FOR** after I am put in charge of making up all laws.

MY OTHER LAWS

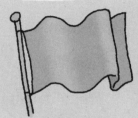

The colors on the NATIONAL FLAG will be changed to LIGHT BROWN, BRUNETTE, and NOT BLOND.

MY face will be on the coins, but only sassy, over-the-shoulder shots.

ONE KEWT DIME

BABY BLUE eyes will officially **NOT** be a big stupid deal any more.

Since I've been listening to them for a while now, it came as no surprise that I'm doing a poster of FATAALD and their new album, which is called *Butter*, after their hit song, "**Butter, Compared 2 U, Girl, Is Margarine.**"

And when they sing it, you can totally tell that they're not singing "you" but the **much cooler** "U." Maybe other people can't tell, but I can. You pick up little things like that when you're in a relationship with a band.

on one of their songs, I heard a BAND AID on the Bass PLAYer's Finger

I sent him a FABULOUS

GET-WELL CARD

Angeline (semi-friend of mine in spite of her **relentless prettiness**) is doing a poster on some band called **The Delicate Sweet Adorable Honey Prissies** or **The Pink Frosted Idiot Weenies** or something like that. I don't know. I never thought of Angeline as somebody who listened to any music other than the angels that sing with pure teary-eyed joy whenever she walks or talks or breathes or whatever, so I wasn't really paying attention.

Isabella (full-time professional best friend) is making a poster for her favorite CD, which isn't really a band but more of a collection of Halloween sound effects. It's just creaking doors and screams, but it has helped her fall asleep since she was five.

Note: Sleepovers at Isabella's? **Not So Much.**

Miss Anderson hangs our work up in the hall for two reasons: **One,** it's a great way for us to become more famous. **And two,** she knows she looks so **fabulous** when she hangs things that the janitors and the men teachers will stop whatever they're doing and do it for her.

There's a very good chance that since my poster will be up in the hall, some set of amazing circumstances could occur where FATAALD will see this poster and hire me to do their album covers. I've seen enough movies about girls to know this is true.

But I need to make sure that the other bands know that I'm not available to do **their** album covers. So I may have to do a poster that is anti-all-other-bands, just to make that clear.

Dear Dumb Diary,

Remember that girl, Vicki Vonder?

No? I've never mentioned her before?

Maybe that's because **nobody has ever mentioned her before.**

Not to anybody. Her name didn't ever even come up in the Vonders' household during dinner conversation between Mr. and Mrs. Vonder.

Mr. Vonder would say, "Hey, our daughter or somebody choked on a seed at lunch."

And Mrs. Vonder would say, "Hey, did you know that mosses and ferns don't have seeds?"

You see? They're more interested in ferns and mosses than their own daughter, and **nobody** is interested in ferns. Even ferns aren't interested in ferns.

vicki

And since I'm talking about seeds, Dumb Diary, here's their deal: You plant one, and it grows slowly. It gets bigger and bigger until maybe a little bud appears on it. Then the bud opens gradually. Plants give you time to prepare yourself for the flower. You might even decide to eat it before it blooms, or pull the petals out of its face one by one to determine if somebody loves you or not.

Some people, however, impolitely **don't** do this. *Some* people will just all of a sudden burst out as a giant magnificent flower without any warning whatsoever.

This is why you know, like, fifty people that you can't stand, but you probably can't name more than one or two flowers that you're mad at right now.

This polite seed I described is exactly the type of seed that Vicki **isn't**. Without warning, she made her pimples go away and she made her hair brush itself and she made her face not always look like it was apologizing for something.

But the worst part of all was — brace yourself — that she was wearing a **FATAALD T-shirt** today. That's **MY** band, so that's technically **MY** shirt.

It's not like I'm selfish. I would probably authorize Isabella to like FATAALD. I might even give Angeline a very limited permit, and Emmily doesn't really matter because she hears whatever she wants to hear whether her headphones are plugged into an Apple iPod or a real apple.

But **NOT** Vicki Vonder. I would not authorize her usage of my band. I needed to talk to somebody about her insult to FATAALD and myself.

mildly upset

So later on, I caught up with Isabella and Angeline, since they are obligated, as friends, to fulfill their duties as complaint receivers. You'll never believe this, but they were offensively listening to a song by FATAALD. **That's right.** And they didn't even consult me about **WHICH** song they should start on.

I mean, it's like nobody respects **Band Ownership** anymore.

Clearly, they should have started on one of FAATALD's earlier songs like **"O Girl, U R a Girl 2 Me"** or maybe **"Hey, Girl, U R So Girltastic"** or even **"U R A Girl. I M Aware of That."**

But no, they had to jump in with the big hit: **"Butter, Compared 2 U, Girl, Is Margarine."**

Butter is pretty much the only dairy product you want to be compared to

I'm delightfully polite, so I didn't even penalize Isabella or Angeline for dating my band behind my back. I just kind of nodded and pleasantly said how great it was that they were into FATAALD.

Angeline said that she thought nobody was more into them than me. This would have been a perfect time for her to have been struck mute — by a medieval throat disease, let's say — but immediately afterward she had to add, "Except maybe for Vicki."

Vicki Vonder? Because of a T-shirt, now we're supposed to believe that SHE is more into my band than me?

I think not.

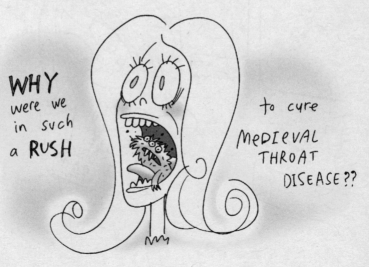

WHY were we in such a RUSH   to cure MEDIEVAL THROAT DISEASE??

In order to prove that *I* was the most into them, I went into the bathroom with a marker and wrote FATAALD on my arm. For good measure, I added the name of their hit, **"BUTTER,"** because I wanted everybody to understand that I know the band **AND** their work.

I wrote it sideways on my left forearm so that when I put it down on my desk, others could read it. That's who needs to know that I'm into this band, after all: **Others.**

At lunch I sat with Emmily, Isabella, and Angeline. We sat across from Hudson Rivers (eighth cutest boy in my grade) and Vicki, who had made the tragic mistake of appearing close to me in her FATAALD T-shirt while I was sporting a far more committed form of adornment: **A MARKER TATTOO.**

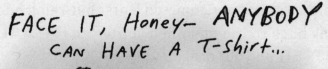

FACE IT, Honey— ANYBODY CAN HAVE A T-shirt...

WORLD'S MEANEST ORTHODONTIST

SPIDER

10 POUNDS OF TURNIPS

But here's the thing about tattoos. (I'd like to direct this to Future Jamie, who may be reading this right now, in the distant future, in case she contemplates getting a real tattoo. . . .)

Dear Future Jamie,

I know you're thinking that a tattoo on your arm would look great dangling out of your rocking convertible spaceship as you drive your genius triplets to summer camp on Mars, but think back. Think back to the day when you wrote **FATAALD BUTTER** on your arm.

Remember how you weren't really thinking about how your tattoo looked? Remember how you didn't notice until the end of lunch that your sleeve hadn't been pulled up far enough, and how Hudson laughed when Vicki stood up and said, "Nice tattoo. **Are you bragging or confessing?**"

And remember when you looked down and realized what it said?

Yeah. That's right. It said, **"FAT BUTT."**

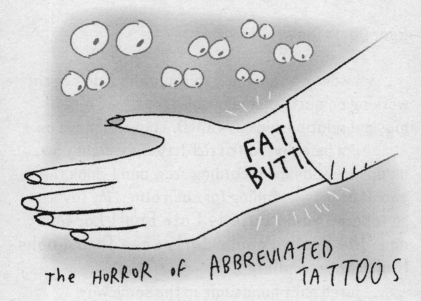

the HORROR of ABBREVIATED TATTOOS

I was late for class trying to wash it off, and I realized as I stood in the girls' bathroom that I had to **break up** with FATAALD. It really hurts me, but I can't see myself having a meaningful relationship with a band that would freely let other girls like their music, and cruelly put me through something like this.

Wednesday 04

Dear Dumb Diary,

I woke up very early this morning and began working on party planning as I considered a new musical relationship. (FATAALD, I have to move on.)

I'm listening to **Jared Jay Fire** right now, an up-and-coming recording star, and I think the two of us may be falling for each other. My favorites so far are **"Kinda Cute Is Cute Enuff For Me"** and **"The Really Popular Girls Lose Their Looks Right After College."**

Jared isn't handsome in the same way FATAALD was handsome. FATAALD always looked a little **dangerous-handsome**, like they might start shoving each other at any moment. Jared looks more **cute-handsome**, like he might give a stuffed animal a chocolate at any moment.

But cute-handsome is still plenty handsome, and FATAALD, I've told you — I. Have. To. Move. On.

I have some serious party planning to do. There's a lot to consider. Originally, I wanted a **beautiful cake**, but I've seen them making beautiful cakes on TV and I've noticed that the more attractive a cake is, the more it's been handled back in the kitchen. I really don't want to eat something thinking about how somebody had practically made out with it.

So I'm going to have a **nice-looking cake**, but not one with a TV career. It will be chocolate, of course, because we all know that a vanilla cake is just a chocolate cake that won't admit what it really wants to be.

At breakfast, Mom reminded me to finish my invitation list, so I immediately grabbed a piece of paper and pen and started listing who I wanted to come. I got all the way down to Isabella, but then I had to **stop and think.**

Am I obligated to invite certain people? Somehow, making it mandatory makes me not want to do it. Like, do I **HAVE** to invite Angeline? I don't have a problem with her anymore — not really — but I'm not sure I never will again. She's a bit like a **blond flu** that I've recovered from, but could get another time.

And do I **HAVE** to invite Hudson? My new relationship with Jared Jay Fire will probably hurt and intimidate him. Which I'm okay with, but his sulking could bring down the party.

Do I **HAVE** to invite Emmily? I love her and everything, but who will explain to her that it isn't **her** birthday?

There's Mike Pinsetti, of course, who is gross and I hate, and Margaret the pencil-chewer, who is gross and I like.

There's Tucker, and Spitty Elizabeth, and that kid who trips over everything. Do they have to come?

PINSETTI

MARGARET

SPITTY ELIZABETH

TUCKER

THAT KID WHO TRIPS OVER EVERYTHING

NADIA

And do I have to invite people that asked me to their parties once? When do those obligations expire? My birthday is, like, three weeks away. How can I be sure I'll even **know** these people that long from now?

The birthday party dynamic is complex. It was wise that we decided to have them no more than once per year. Fortunately, I have Jared Jay Fire's love ballad, **"Stupid Ain't As Stupid When It's U,"** to calm me down.

Oh, Jared, you always know just what to **whine**.

Oh
Sweet
Sugar
Honey sweet
Honey
Sweetheart
you are
high in
CaLoRiES

Thursday 05

Dear Dumb Diary,

Thursday is always **Meat Loaf Day** at our school. I know what you're thinking, but don't be too hasty: Meat loaf is a wholesome and delicious food that is a favorite everywhere with hungry young middle-school bacteria.

Non-bacteria, however, don't care for it so much.

And by "don't care for it," I really mean "makes them vomit out their ears."

It's just that "don't care for it" is a **classier** way to say it, and I'm all about **classy**.

Like today when I noticed, like, at least **forty people** that were listening to FATAALD.

Some were putting a FATAALD sticker on their locker, or writing the band name on their jeans or notebooks. Don't worry: I classfully didn't laugh at them scornfully.

The classy thing to do was to just **smile mockingly**, and so that's what I did.

I'm not sure if I was directing the smile at my fellow pitiful students, or if it was really directed more at FATAALD, who now — since I've left them — are playing to a much more shallow and uninformed listener.

me, smiling mockingly

Margaret, chewing chewfully

Angeline seemed rather surprised when I told her that I was music-dating Jared Jay Fire now. I think everybody assumed that FATAALD and I were going to grow old together, and we really should have. I can picture them playing their **really old guitars** and me twitching to the music.

But things change. People change. We have to accept it when people and their bands get divorced. The important thing is to remain mature about it, and never forget the good times.

Also, blaming Vicki Vonder for it seems to comfort me. I recommend that others use Vicki for **blaming on.**

UNICORNS AREN'T REAL. How can we be sure that's not Vicki's fault as well?))

excellent question

At dinner, I told my parents that I really only liked Jared Jay Fire now and it made my dad choke on the **Stuff-and-Things-in-Something-Sauce** Mom had prepared for dinner.

Dad always chokes on Mom's cooking — we all do — so it wasn't unusual, but there was something about Dad's discharge that struck me as different. Probably because Dad's discharge actually **struck me**.

Usually, he has time to get his napkin up in front of his mouth, but for some reason, this came as such a total surprise to him that I got nailed by a little dinner spew.

He's probably just really excited that I've found a whole bunch of new songs to play loudly.

HORK

mom's food is only SLIGHTLY more gross when served to you this way

After dinner we watched some TV, and we saw this little girl playing a violin while she bounced on a pogo stick while being really pretty.

But here's the thing: *She's waaaaay younger than I am.*

My whole life, it's never bothered me when people OLDER than me could do things that I couldn't. I always figured that they could do those things because they had all that extra time to learn.

But now I see violin-playing-pogo-stick girl and other youngsters accomplishing things that I can't do. I've just been assuming that these children have some sort of mental disease that makes them **yearn to annoy**.

I think maybe I've been wrong. Maybe our birthdays mean more than just getting presents. They might also mean that I have to start accomplishing **more and more** to make up for my advancing age, which will soon begin to make me **more and more gross**.

(I think I may have just realized why accomplishments are so important to adults. They distract you from their wrinkly nastiness.)

And just coming up with a device that can knock a little violinist off her pogo stick might be satisfying, but it won't be enough. I have to come up with some sort of **Super-Incredible Accomplishment** by my birthday.

my invention of an improved mousetrap, which is improved because it's not after mice.

Friday 06

Dear Dumb Diary,

Okay, now this is just sad. Today at school, Vicki was wearing her FATAALD shirt again. But that's not all. **So was Emmily.**

I asked Emmily if she made the shirt herself, perhaps while she was wearing it and looking in the mirror, but she insisted that she had not and that she bought it at "the fancy store."

On top of that, Isabella had written FATAALD on her hand in marker, which I pointed out was a big mistake. It had taken me about **forty washes** to get my arm tattoo off, and I presented my very pink arm to Isabella as proof.

She said she wasn't worried because her grandma had some medicine that would take it right off if she hadn't drunk all of it already.

I also pointed out that Isabella was kind of getting FATAALD on the rebound, because I had already broken up with them, and that makes her look desperate.

I don't know why this seemed like a good idea...

Two thoughts:

One: School lockers seem to have been designed to create the maximum banging noise when you are slammed up against one, which makes me think that they were probably engineered by somebody who was a bully when they were a child.

And two: You really never get used to how fast Isabella can grab your collar. She could snatch a ham sandwich out of a cobra's mouth. (Do cobras eat those? They probably eat those.)

Isabella, it turns out, is not super-okay with looking desperate, I guess.

"I'm just trying to be happy," she said, and I apologized right away because especially at that very second, with her fingers around my windpipe, I agreed it would be a really, really great idea if she was happy.

Happy people are less **chokey-to-deathy**.

If **copying me** makes Isabella happy, I can live with that. A little. For now.

It's time for me to sign off for the evening, because I'm thinking about having a theme for my birthday party, and I have to get to work. Here are a few possibilities:

KOALA PARTY!

Everybody comes dressed as their favorite KOALA AND WE DO KOALA-RELATED ACTIVITIES.

I don't think we are supposed to eat EUCALYPTUS LEAVES.

NINJA PARTY!

Everybody shows up Dressed as a NINJA...
... OR DO THEY????

ADULT PARTY!

Everybody shows up dressed as an ADULT AND Rests until it's time to Go Home and rest.

Saturday 07

Dear Dumb Diary,

Isabella asked me to come over today. I figured it was probably to apologize for roughing me up yesterday, but then I remembered that Isabella only apologizes when there is a judge or policeman in the room.

And when there are no **unlocked exits**.

Instead, she wanted to help me plan my birthday party, because she isn't allowed to have one ever since the very first party she had in kindergarten.

Isabella told everybody who she invited that she was a **twin**. She said that her sister, who was named Monella, couldn't come to school because she had been mauled by a bear as an infant and needed a special toilet that schools couldn't afford, but they should also bring a birthday gift for her anyway. Or a lot of money.

Monella isn't really a name. It means **"brat"** in Italian, and it was what Isabella's grandma always called her. So when her parents saw some of the presents with the words "To Monella" on them, they just figured that Isabella was using the nickname at school.

They never would have figured it out, except that one of the parents asked to **meet Monella.**

ISABELLA   MONELLA   **39**

Good thing Isabella doesn't mind being spanked.

You have to admit that it was a really clever scheme because if those parents *hadn't* asked, then Isabella would have gotten double the presents. She might have gotten double the presents for **the rest of her life**, if she had kept it going.

But in the end, I suppose it was sort of a bad plan after all, because her parents never let her have another one. (Another party, not another spanking. They did let her have more of those. All she could ever hope for.)

SPANKMATIC

I'm surprised her parents never invented this

Isabella and I agreed not to discuss FATAALD, and focused on my birthday party instead.

She said that we should try to figure out who will bring the **best gifts** and divide that by who will **eat the least**. I couldn't bring myself to stop her because that formula was the closest thing to math I've ever seen her do.

She had created a graph of some of the skinniest and richest kids at school to help me choose.

I told her that this was **such** a wrong way to look at things. I mean, sometimes skinny kids eat a lot and sometimes chubby kids eat very little. Heck, manatees eat nothing but salad and swim every day, and look at them.

Yuck. Shouldn't a charity get them some Ranch Dressing for this junk?

Isabella said that I owe it to myself to pick at least one of these kids, because it will help offset the low-quality gift she is planning to give me, as well as her obscene appetite.

I finally agreed to her plan and told her to just pick somebody for me, since she was probably the only one that could fully comprehend her **greed-based math.**

ISABELLA'S MATH

GUEST'S WEIGHT:	200 POUNDS
THIS GUEST GIVES GIFTS OF THIS VALUE :	$10.00
KID WILL EAT 1.5% OF HIS WEIGHT, VALUED AT —	$5.00
OVERALL VALUE OF THIS GUEST—	$ 5.00

We also made a **Temporary List of People Who Could Possibly Maybe Get Invited Pending a Final Decision,** along with the pros and cons of inviting them.

POSSIBLE GUEST	PRO	CON
MISS BRUNTFORD	MIGHT TRIP ON THE STAIRS	MIGHT ATTRACT GORILLAS
AUNT CAROL	ALTHOUGH OLD, STILL FUN	OLD
A CLOWN	MIGHT MAKE BALLOON ANIMALS	MIGHT SWALLOW GUESTS' SOULS
GORILLA	MIGHT COMICALLY MAUL CLOWN	MIGHT ATTRACT MISS BRUNTFORD

And we discussed **other themes** that Isabella liked.

ISABELLA'S PARTY THEMES

The "LET'S GIVE JAMIE'S BIRTHDAY PRESENTS TO HER MOST AGGRESSIVE FRIEND" Theme.

The "CAN ISABELLA EAT AN ENTIRE BIRTHDAY CAKE? LET'S WATCH AND LEARN" Theme.

The "Let's give her Jamie's Christmas presents while we're at it" Theme

We started talking about the music we should play at the party, but I quickly realized this could be a very sore subject, especially since I'm now involved with a very exciting recording star and Isabella is dragging around that one band that is **so uncool** that they don't even have a name.

Seriously? Just initials? How lame is that? Don't make me LOL.

Okay, I miss them a little.

Sunday 08

Dear Dumb Diary,

Aunt Carol stopped by with Angeline today. They were going shopping together **AGAIN**. Angeline never buys anything, but since Aunt Carol is married to Angeline's Uncle Dan, she is legally obligated to recognize Angeline as her niece. So she often does degrading acts of charity like spending time with her.

They invited me to join them, but since it's Sunday I have a ton of homework to finish. Angeline, obviously not fully understanding **WHY** Sunday was inserted into the week, finishes her homework early and thereby has to struggle to find ways to kill time on Sunday, such as **doing things** or **having fun**.

it must be MISERABLE to be This Free on a SUNDAY.

I feel only pity

After they left, I spent some time worrying about my life's progress, because I had put it down on my To-Do List:

Sunday, 2:00–2:15: Worry about life's progress.

By that, I meant I worried about needing to **accomplish something** before my birthday. That little violin-playing-pogo-stick girl had really gotten to me.

Maybe a letter to the TV station would help.

Dear T.V.,
please stop broadcasting stories of maniac children proving how great they are. You are just making humanity angry.
Best wishes,
Jamie Kelly

P.S. My hand is actually much prettier than this but hands can be hard to draw.

That probably won't help, because there is still a chance I could see that girl or somebody like her in a magazine or online. Even though I've tried to contact the entire **big, hairy Internet** before, they never respond.

I said to myself that I have to be better than everybody at something, or at least keep up with little bratty pogo-stickers, and that no matter what it took, I would sacrifice anything to accompl —

Then it was 2:15 and time to move on.

After dinner, I went up to my room and put on my headphones and really got down with some Jared Jay Fire.

I also **Broke It Loose, Got Busy,** and at one point, I even **Shook It Like I Stole It.**

Jared, you're great, but not great for the homework. See if you can tell the exact moment while I was writing this report where I broke, got, and shook.

Monday 09

Dear Dumb Diary,

So Jared and I decided to go public today, and in art class I told Miss Anderson and the world that I wanted to change my poster selection from **old what's-their-name** to Jared Jay Fire.

This was met by hushed gasps — so hushed, in fact, that they couldn't be heard. Still, I know there was **gasping**. And a snicker or two, since boys are very jealous of pop stars and tend to make fun of them, as if they know anything about music.

Seriously, many of the boys at my school can't name three bands, but can play the entire Mario Brothers theme flawlessly on their armpits.

Miss Anderson said, "That's okay. Our interests can change. Last week, Angeline and a few others switched their poster project to some band called FatAl or something, and now this."

WAIT. THEY CHANGED TO FATAALD?

I looked over at Angeline, who just grinned. Isabella never looked up from her poster. Emmily proudly held up a big, **upside-down F**, which I believe was either the first letter in her FATAALD poster or what we all assumed was the grade she would be getting on it.

I want to visit Emmily's world one Day...

for I'm sure the cockroaches look like UNICORNS

I cornered Angeline over by the pencil sharpener and warned her.

"Isabella is **band-dating** FATAALD," I said. "Don't you think it's a little low-down for you to go and be a big fan of theirs, especially right under her nose?"

Angeline whirled around. I'm sure she was hoping to **clobber me** with a big face full of her magical blond hair, but I'm not exactly new to her whirls, and I dodged it.

"Maybe you don't know everything, okay, Jamie?" she said, and I immediately began to object, because let's face it, **I almost do**.

But mid-objection, I suddenly decided to keep quiet. I looked back at Isabella, who was maintaining a very brave face in spite of the fact that Angeline was out to steal her band.

It was such a brave face that it closely resembled an **I-Don't-Even-Care** face, but that's probably because Isabella has learned brave faces from me.

MY EXTREMELY BRAVE FACES

FACE USED WHEN POLAR BEAR ATTACKS.

FACE USED WHEN DINOSAUR ATTACKS WITH FLAMING ARROWS.

FACE USED WHEN DAD TRIMS HIS NASTY THICK TOENAILS. (I KNOW, BUT THEY ARE REALLY SCARY)

Tuesday 10

Dear Dumb Diary,

A long time ago, I wrote a letter to the president about the space program and how it would be a good idea for **me** to select the people that should be shot into space.

I made a lot of very good points about who should be selected, such as weight, ease of stuffing into a bag and tossing into a rocket, unnatural blondness of hair, and how much happier our Earth would be as a result.

I was much younger when I wrote it, and I understand that this would not have been seriously considered.

But that was six months ago, and I think now I am **qualified** to choose — and I'm choosing Vicki Vonder.

it's simple!

1. INSERT OFFENSIVE PERSON
2. PRESS LAUNCH BUTTON
3. ENJOY YOUR IMPROVED WORLD!

Today she was **actually walking around** with a Jared Jay Fire T-shirt on! I think it's safe to assume that she's somehow spying on me and Jared, the exact same way she spied on me and FATAALD.

So I confronted her about it.

"Nice shirt," I said, clearly implying that she had no right to wear it.

"Thanks," she said, pretending to totally miss what I was clearly implying.

"Been a fan long?" I said, clearly implying that there was a very real threat that I might **pounce on her like a puma** and shred her shirt with my razor-sharp puma claws.

"Nope. Just started listening to him," she said, possibly not knowing what a puma was.

"Yeah. Well. See you later," I said, clearly implying now that, in addition to a puma, I could also go all grizzly bear on her. But frankly, my puma is better, so I'm not surprised she didn't really pick up on the grizzly thing I was laying down.

my puma thing

My moose thing
(I never use this one)

But c'mon. Why are you copying me again?
Seriously, Vicki, **what's next?**

my awesome walk?

my awesome HAIR?

my awesome fashion?

my awesome Beagle?

Wednesday 11

Dear Dumb Diary,

Okay. Okay. **GET THIS.**

So today, Emmily is listening to Jared Jay Fire on her iPod. How do I know? Because Emmily loudly sings along to her iPod. Once you understand how Emmily **misunderstands** the song lyrics, you can figure out the song she's listening to.

For example, when Emmily sang "Olive beagles in disguise," I know she was attempting to sing, "I love eagles in the sky," which is a line from Jared's hit **"I Love Eagles in the Sky but Not as Much as U, Girl."**

Yeah, I know. It's not easy. For a while last year she was singing, "We washed you a hairy gross mess." It wasn't until she stopped singing it in January that we figured out it was **"We Wish You a Merry Christmas."**

FLARBLE NARBLE GLOOB

Later on, I was walking past Isabella's locker and noticed that she had a picture of Jared taped up on the inside of the door.

Of course, **I confronted her**.

"Nice picture," I said.

"Are you doing the puma thing on me?" she asked, demonstrating her mastery of detecting pumas.

"**What?** No, I'm just saying that it's a nice picture," I said, skillfully lying about what I had just been doing.

Isabella turned her head so that the glare off her glasses blocked her eyes. She always knows the exact right angle to position her head so you can't see her eyes. That **eyelessness** is something that can make a puma back the heck down.

"So, uh, have you broken up with FATAALD?" I asked, less pumaishly, though even angrier.

"Staying happy," she said with a wink.

Well, I assume there was a wink. I still couldn't see her eyes. I think I heard a wink under there.

At dinner tonight, Dad asked if I was still into Jared Jay Fire, which was weird because he is generally not interested in the kind of **amazing** music that I'm interested in.

Since he is very, very old, he only likes a certain category of song — songs that he can sing along to while he bangs on the steering wheel to inform other drivers that:

1. He likes the music he is listening to.
2. He can't sing.
3. They are bad songs.
4. He has decided to **embarrass his daughter to death**, and he is really prepared to throw his neck out of joint in order to do it.

SOUNDS LiKE PAiN BUT is pure happiness

It got even weirder when I told Dad that I didn't like Jared Jay Fire anymore. He actually looked disappointed. Seriously, Dad, **man up** a little. How attached could you have gotten to him in few days?

Then Mom started talking about some singer she liked when she was younger and how cute he was, and she said that maybe I'd like him, too. You know, if liking a singer my mom found cute didn't make my **flesh crawl**.

And then it suddenly occurred to me. My crawling flesh made it clear. I don't know why I didn't see it before:

I'm better than everyone.

Knowing that my mom likes a singer makes it impossible for me to enjoy his music, in much the same way — but opposite — that Vicki and Isabella and Angeline and Emmily are copying me: They want so badly to be like me.

I'm just like them, only better, and *they know that*. And they're copying me.

Now I just have to prove it.

CAN INSTANTLY IDENTIFY GREAT MUSIC.

IS ALWAYS NICE TO GROSS PEOPLE WHO DON'T REALLY DESERVE NICENESS.

HAS MEMORIZED ALL CUTE ANIMALS.

WILL EVENTUALLY DO SOMETHING BETTER THAN ANYBODY (MY AGE).

OF **COURSE** they want to COPY ME!

Thursday 12

Dear Dumb Diary,

Last night, I asked Mom all about this singer she liked. His name is Verge Aplo.

(I know, I know.)

I downloaded a picture of him and glued it to my notebook, and Mom was **really really really really really** happy to help.

I also downloaded a couple of his big hits, including **"You're a Rock-and-Roll Kiss Machine, Baby"** and **"Baby, I Wanna Kiss You and Rock and Roll and Kiss."**

Jeez. How dumb did song titles used to be? Who spells out the word **"you"**?

VERGE

really mom?
really?

This morning, I made sure that everybody saw the notebook, especially Vicki. Her face pretended not to be interested, but I could tell that her eyes were very committed to seeing the picture and memorizing the name, which I helpfully highlighted in one of my more effective **glitter blends**. It's equal parts Fairy Gold, Moonglo Silver, and sugar. I formulated this mix specifically to burn into the memory. Plus, in an emergency, it can be used for food.

At lunch, Angeline immediately picked up my binder when I sat down.

"Verge Aplo?" she asked. "Verge?" She said it as though Verge might be a skin condition.

"Yeah. **He's the greatest**," I told her in a tone that suggested I was telling a very special chimpanzee something it should have learned long ago.

"Is **he** your new favorite? He's replacing Jared Jay Fire?" Angeline asked.

"Yeah," I said as I stood up. "We're very happy together." I tried to whip my hair around like Angeline does, but missed her and managed to whip Miss Bruntford, our six-hundred-pound cafeteria monitor, in the face instead.

Hitting Miss Bruntford with your hair would typically result in detention, or having to help pick up trash in the cafeteria, or at the very least a **strong compulsion** to burn your own hair off. But Bruntford just stood there, making a sound like air escaping from a punctured parade balloon.

For a second I felt **bad**, as if I had really hurt her. Then I felt **good**, as if I had really hurt her.

Then I realized what was going on.

She was grinning and squealing, but when you're her age, your squealer is practically never used, and it gets rusty and wheezy.

She was staring at my notebook. She was staring at **Verge Aplo.**

I had to move before anybody else saw it. After all, having a relationship with a singer that Bruntford was having a relationship with would be **disastrous**.

"Can I go?" I asked her, and she nodded kindly. Her oversized head was doubtlessly filled with memories of listening to Verge Aplo when she was just a calf.

By the end of the day, I noticed that Isabella had taken down her Jared Jay Fire picture, and Emmily was singing something that may have been a Verge Aplo song. Or maybe she had just stubbed her toe. **Anybody's guess.**

But I really think that they're switching to Verge. **They're copying me.**

Could this all be just from the picture on my binder? Or is somebody spying on me another way?

HEY! COPY JAMIE KELLY, EVERYBODY!

DISTINCTIVE HAIR WIG

ADORABLE SEW-ON HEARTS FOR YOUR SHIRT

BEAGLE PEW

JUG OF ODOR SAUCE TO DUMP ON YOUR PET.

JUST KIDDING. STOP COPYING ME.

FRIDAY 13

Dear Dumb Diary,

My mom had Verge playing when I came down to breakfast this morning.

My dad was kind of nodding along and asking me how groovy I thought the song was. (Yeah. He really and truly said, **"Groovy."** Not kidding.)

Check out a few other things my dad says:

LAWN CARE IS RADICAL!

This is as COOL AS A BALANCED DIET!

AWESOME EXTREMENESS, YOUNGSTERS!

RESPONSIBILITY ROCKS!

DAD'S UNCOOLNESS ACTUALLY HURTS MY FEELINGS A LITTLE

Before the first bell at school, I could feel people staring at my binder, checking to see if Verge Aplo and I were still an item.

I secretly peeked around a corner and saw Angeline, who was listening to her iPod by her locker, flash Isabella this gesture:

That's right. Angeline flashed a "V-A."
<u>V</u>erge <u>A</u>plo.

That's who she was listening to!
She flashed the initials right in my face while she
didn't know my face was there, so it's insulting on
two levels, really.

When you insult
me behind my
back, you deprive
me of **MY RIGHT**
to give you a dirty
look **WHICH I**
can't do with my
BACK—believe
me, I'VE **TRIED**

Best I can do →

And there you have it. I do something, they copy it. What more proof do you need?

It's infuriating, but maybe this could be my violin-playing-pogo-stick girl accomplishment. Although, do I really want to be the **World's Most Copied Person**?

I guess that title might make me less angry about it, and if something that used to make you crazy angry suddenly doesn't anymore, it becomes **unfuriating**. Is that enough?

INFURIATED   UNFURIATED

70

Saturday 14

Dear Dumb Diary,

I made my party invitations today. The ones you buy at the store are fine, but when you make them yourself, you send a very important message to the recipients: I care enough about you to show you what your crafting skills really **should** be.

Here's what they look like:

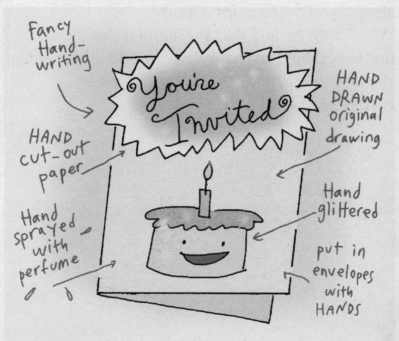

Fancy Hand-writing

HAND cut-out paper

Hand sprayed with perfume

You're Invited

HAND DRAWN original drawing

Hand glittered

put in envelopes with HANDS

Isabella came over to help since they were spraying for **bedbugs** at her house. Her mom found one in her mean older brothers' room. Isabella's mom hates anything that crawls, so it meant that her brothers had to completely clean their room from top to bottom, which took four days, and then take their beds totally apart and carry the parts outside for her mom to cover with insecticide.

It will take a couple days for the new mattresses to be delivered, so her brothers will be sleeping on the floor for a while.

Isabella said that the moral is that her brothers should not have eaten the donut they knew she was saving, and that it was **the best bedbug she ever bought.**

not everybody knows where you can buy a bedbug

Isabella helped write the addresses on the party invitations and stamp them. I had this idea to make Stinker lick the envelopes by putting just a little bit of peanut butter on them, but Isabella wound up licking the peanut butter off instead. When Isabella smells peanut butter, she gets as **slobberish** as a beagle.

While we were working, Isabella asked several times about Verge Aplo. She wanted to know who he was and why I liked him. Since Isabella is my very best friend, it seemed like the best thing to do was to **lie**.

Verge, I told her, is a self-taught guitar player who grew up so poor that his guitar only had one string, and he had to keep tightening and loosening it really quick just to play a song.

You have to admit. This WOULD Be impressive.

I went on to say that his family couldn't even afford paper for him to write his music on, so to compose, Verge had to arrange tadpoles on lines he scratched in the dirt.

Isabella asked why he didn't just scratch the notes as well, but I explained that he had to change them around sometimes. Now that I think of it, he could have just used stones, I guess. But tadpoles look like notes, so that's why I said tadpoles.

I explained to her that his very first song, **"Ain't No Koala Back Girl,"** was written for a **pet teacup koala** he had when he was growing up in Australia, which was swallowed when his aunt accidentally drank from the teacup it was sleeping in.

Isabella said that pets like teacup poodles are only called that because of their size and not because they live in teacups. I told her she was mostly right, but everything is different in Australia, as is clearly evidenced by the giant Labrador retrievers that they have hopping all over the place with baby Labrador retrievers sticking out of their pouches. I reminded her that **"kangaroo"** is Australian for Labrador retriever.

Isabella didn't look completely convinced, so I added that one time Verge was attacked by a platypus with rabies and had to battle it with nothing but a grilled cheese sandwich. When the Australian dust cleared, there was nothing left but a platypus toenail. Verge honored the fierce creature by using that toenail as a **guitar pick** on every song he ever wrote after that.

I know she could have checked any of this out, but looking things up feels like homework to Isabella, so I'm confident that there is no chance of that ever happening.

By the time she left, she was a huge Verge Aplo fan. **Without ever hearing his music.**

Isabella doesn't cook because it reminds her of chemistry which reminds her of school.

Isabella doesn't make her bed because it reminds her of cooking which reminds her of chemistry.

Isabella doesn't do anything she doesn't like because it reminds her of making her bed which reminds her of cooking.

Sunday 15

Dear Dumb Diary,

Planning the menu for my birthday party took a lot of thought. I had to choose between the vast variety of things my friends like to eat, such as:

PIZZA

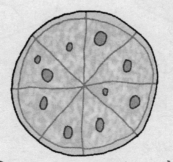

PIZZA with, Like, ONE THING ON IT

Adults often dismiss pizza as an inadequate food, but when you analyze it, you'll find that it's essentially **perfect**.

It has all of the major food groups represented: dairy, vegetables, grains, and even fiber, if you get some hair in your mouth while you're eating it. Like all circular foods, it's delicious, and it promotes math by making you count how many pieces you've had and how many you're entitled to based on how many people are sharing the pizza.

And if you tell people the pepperonis remind you of scabs, they'll probably give you all of their pepperonis. **Maybe for life.**

Liver

Sock

Brussels Sprout

See? You've never seen these gross foods in circle form.

Which reminds me: I want to make sure to remember when I grow up and am a mom (like one of those moms that is so pretty you're surprised to learn that they are one) to always buy furniture and carpet and everything for my awesome Hollywood mansion that are all the same color as the foods my kids will tend to drop.

I'll probably also dress them only in those colors.

Although I guess there's a risk that they'll only like stew, and I don't want to live in a **stew-colored** house. Maybe what I'll do is only let them know about foods that make good carpet colors. Or I'll only let them eat **clear foods**.

Mommy, I dropped my clear sandwich and I can't find it...

That's okay. The clear dog will eat it.

We used to play games at birthday parties, but now, not so much.

At a big holiday thing, a game like bobbing for apples is fine, but at our advanced level of maturity, suggesting a game like pin the tail on the donkey at a birthday party would be regarded as **rudely babyish**.

I wonder if maybe there's a market for games I could create just for the more mature middle schooler's birthday party. I'll have to give this some thought. Maybe that could be my accomplishment! I could be the first person to invent **non-lame party games** for older kids.

COMPETITIVE COMPLAINING ABOUT PARENTS

COMPETITIVE ACNE

BOINK

9.5 8.5 7.5

COMPETITIVE REFUSING TO COMPETE

Yeah, maybe not.

Monday 16

Dear Dumb Diary,

AH–HA! (Written very loudly.)
Today in art class, Miss Anderson asked how everybody was doing on their projects. I brilliantly bent over to tie my shoe at that exact moment, so that there was no way she would call on me first.

I had to tie and retie my shoes several times, since she wound up calling on a few people before she called on THE PRECISE PEOPLE I NEEDED TO ANSWER HER QUESTION AND COMMIT TO A BAND.

if you stay out of a teacher's field of view, they will forget that you exist.

FINALLY, she called on Vicki, who said that she was changing her band again, this time to Verge Aplo. Angeline and Isabella nodded in agreement. Emmily just leaned over and whispered that she could help me learn to tie shoes faster.

Miss Anderson chuckled, because she's an **experienced teacher** and experienced teachers know that chuckling at students when you're annoyed won't get you fired, but screaming at them might. Also, experienced teachers have learned to disable that part of the brain that cares about most things.

Miss Anderson looked at me and raised her eyebrows way above her eyes, which are eyelined so perfectly that her eyes look like o's in parentheses. (o)(o). (Except that parentheses go the wrong way.) Her expression clearly asked: *Jamie, have you also changed your mind?*

eye parentheses going the right way

"Well, yes." I said casually. "I'm also doing mine on Verge Aplo," I added, even casualler.

"Verge?" Miss Anderson asked.

"Yes," I said, and I think I heard some minds blow a little bit. They all know I'm kind of a **hip, fast-lane girl** and were clearly surprised that I still liked the same performer for this long. **(Five days.)**

"Whatever," Miss Anderson said. I guess hers was not one of the blown minds I heard.

I sat back down and started doing some small sketches in the traditional position that indicates to others that they should not try to see what I'm doing, but always has just the **opposite effect.**

Nothing says "COME HAVE A LOOK AT THIS"

Like "YOU CAN'T HAVE A LOOK AT THIS"

Finally, Angeline slid over and started questioning me.

"So, it's **Verge Aplo**, huh?" she asked.

"Yes," I said cutely.

"Not Jared anymore?" she asked.

"**Verge Aplo**," I said again, even cuter than before (which I know is **hard to believe**).

"And not FATAALD?" she asked.

"**Vergey**," I said. Then I smiled at her with all the cuteness I had been storing up in my face, which was a lot because my face is like a cuteness camel that can hold a ton of cuteness in its cuteness hump.

← So cute!

Angeline looked at me the way some teachers (and all police) look at Isabella — like I was hiding something. I found that insulting, because I'm not. As far as she knows.

If you really are my friend, Angeline, you'll believe me when I tell you things, whether they're **true or not.**

AS MY FRIEND, YOU ARE LEGALLY

OBLIGATED TO BELIEVE

- I SAW A UFO ONE TIME.

- THAT WAS MY LAST PIECE OF GUM.

- I'M PRETTY SURE I SAW THE PRESIDENT AT A GAS STATION IN CUTOFFS.

- LAY OFF ABOUT THE GUM ALREADY, I TOLD YOU IT WAS MY LAST PIECE.

PURE HONESTY

When I got home, Mom asked if I wanted to listen to some new Verge Aplo song she got. I said sure, because he's just the greatest and hardly looks like a **complete weirdo** on his album covers.

Turns out I could have stopped at **"sure"** and probably will stop there in the future, because even though I am up in my room with the door shut, Mom is playing the music so loud that it's making my ears hurt. But it's making my nose hurt more because it's also making the dogs fart, which I think probably strongly resembles what a Verge Aplo song would remind you of **if you could smell one**.

Tuesday 17

Dear Dumb Diary,

As you know, I've been faking my love for Verge, and that is why I am writing this so quietly right now. I must carefully guard the identity of my new musical relationship from **you-know-who**, or I'm going to have to **you-know-what** in her **you-know-where**.

I actually have no idea what the **you-know-what** or **you-know-where** is, but it sounds beautifully threatening. The **you-know-who** is Angeline. Or maybe Vicki. Or Isabella. Or Emmily. Or all of them and more.

It's more of a **you-know-whos**, I guess.

I only suspect everybody.

I want to go on record as saying that my new band relationship is with this band called the **Whisker Brothers,** which is funny because I'm pretty sure they don't shave yet. They are handsome in that way where you know that they would also be pretty if they dressed up like girls, and they're hardly bad at singing, and sometimes you see them on TV shows that are only a little bit horrible, so I don't think I will have any reason to be ashamed when I reveal that they are MY BAND in art class.

The Whisker Brothers

I'm going to wait until next Monday to announce my change, so that copycats will simply not have enough time to change their posters.

What they do after this assignment doesn't concern me much since Miss Anderson will put these posters up in the hall, and that will pretty much make the Whisker Brothers officially **mine and mine alone.**

Getting hung up in the hall makes it official. It's like you and your poster got married.

Let's face it.

He's a **VERY** LUCKY POSTER

As long as I don't tell anybody who they are, this band is mine. And since all of the other posters will be of different bands, the Whisker Brothers will be mine and mine forever.

I'm laughing in a **really dangerous, crazy** kind of way, Dumb Diary. I really wish you had ears to hear this.

Wait. I'll draw you ears.

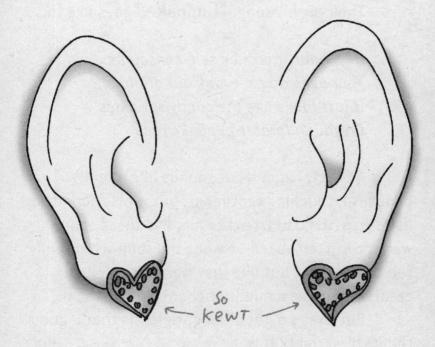

← So kewt →

See? Crazy, right?

Wednesday 18

Dear Dumb Diary,

Yeah, so I secretly spent some time with the Whisker Brothers in my ears today. I worked really hard to enjoy their songs, because that's what a relationship is about: **putting up with somebody.**

Their big hit song, "**Cupcake,**" goes like this:

Hey, babe, don't be self-conscious.
Your acne doesn't look out of place.
It just looks like the candy sprinkles
On your adorable cupcake face.

At first, I know that sounds like a really beautiful, touching sentiment, but it also sounds a little **manufactured** to me, like these songs weren't written based on what the songwriter really felt at the time, but like they were especially created to make a middle-school girl like them.

But that's a good thing, right? Is that a good thing? It is, right? It is.

Let's say that it is. Much better than FATAALD, right?

Thursday 19

Dear Dumb Diary,

Meat Loaf Day.
I sat down at lunch with my tray, and after trying to squeeze down a couple bites, I felt Angeline staring at me. And grinning. Vicki was grinning at me, too. And Bruntford was grinning at me.

I became aware of a sound you would imagine a rhinoceros might make if you dragged it out of a sewer by its tail. Set to music.

"What IS that?" I said.

It turns out that Bruntford was encouraged, I guess, by the number of kids with Verge Aplo written on their notebooks and hands and jeans. So she had a special treat for us today. **She played his music in the cafeteria.**

I realized that since I'm supposed to be totally his biggest fan and everything, I should have recognized it. Angeline immediately seemed to pick up on the fact that I had not.

"You don't recognize your **Vergey**?" she asked snotfully.

"Oh, sure! Of course. I was just distracted a little," I said, pointing over at Bruntford, who was now swinging her ample rear end back and forth like a couple of pickle barrels hanging from a crane.

Still, it seemed like Angeline didn't totally believe me, and I don't know why. I mean, Bruntford was distracting **everybody**. You could almost hear every kid in the cafeteria say a quiet private prayer to **never ever ever** grow up.

Busting a move

into little pieces

I started bobbing my head to the music (a task made easier by the gagging reflex the meat loaf brings on) and making my **"This music is awesome"** face while Angeline made her **"I'm not sure I believe you"** face and Emmily made her **"There is food on my face"** face.

Other Well-Known Faces...

Staying Awake in Class FACE

School picture FACE

Thanks, Grandma, for the sports bra FACE

The sports bra conversation is going to continue FACE

Friday 20

Dear Dumb Diary,

Miss Anderson wants us to work on our music posters in school **only**, and not take them home. If we do that, she'll need to come up with something to teach us about art during class, and when teachers have to come up with a new lesson off the top of their heads, you're not going to like it. The last time this happened, she just read us the names of all the colors in a box of crayons.

So I worked in Miss Anderson's room at lunch today, instead of eating in the cafeteria. Miss Anderson let me do this because I explained that I had to do a little of that ***top secret extra work I need to do***, and I'm pretty much her star pupil.

When I asked her permission she said, "Yes, please do." Or maybe, "I'd love that, Jamie," or probably, "See if I care."

Sepia, Indigo, Periwinkle, Meat loaf, Fuchsia, Scarlet.....

Anyway, my poster requires some **special features** to defeat the copycats, and I need to do some of the work in secret. I can't tell you exactly what these features are now, because, frankly, Dumb Diary, I'm not sure if maybe the copycats could be sneaking into my room and reading you in search of my **secret plans**, like when Isabella read you and told everybody about that one time I had no clean laundry and I wore a pair of my mom's underwear to school and it felt like I had a tablecloth down my pants all day.

NO! SORRY, DUMB DIARY— YOU CAN'T SEE THE TOP SECRET FEATURES!

Oh! And on the subject of massive underthings, here's something interesting and nightmarish: I still can't get the image of Bruntford's dancing out of my mind. Same goes for the grinning. You don't know how much you miss being **snarled** at by a Bigfoot until one day it **grins and dances** at you.

Maybe I can be the youngest person ever to track down a Bigfoot and make it stop dancing. Imagine the gratitude of the forest creatures.

I wonder if violin-playing-pogo-stick brat could **top that**.

Saturday 21

Dear Dumb Diary,

Today, Dad shook me awake and said that I was talking in my sleep, mumbling something about who was the **greatest band in the world** but he couldn't understand what I was saying and he wanted to know.

I told him that I couldn't remember my dream because a crazy man shook me out of it.

He apologized and sat down in a chair next to my bed and ordered me to go back to sleep and dream it again and talk in my sleep again, but do it **more clearly** this time.

See, there's crazy, and then there's **DADCRAZY**.

Dadcrazy is a special kind of crazy, because you know he's probably not dangerous, but he also can't be reasoned with.

A regular crazy person, like one who thinks he's a hamster or something, can probably be reasoned with. You can get one of those balls you let hamsters roll around in and invite him to play in it. About twenty minutes later, after he realizes he can't even stuff his big human head inside, he'll probably be ready to accept that he's **not a hamster**.

Dads won't listen to this sort of logic. A dad who believed he was a hamster would tell you that you had a defective hamster ball. Then he'd offer to drive you to the pet store to find one that worked, never even acknowledging that hamsters can't drive. Or buy things. Or use the word **"defective."**

I could have tried to explain to Dad why I couldn't just fall asleep and dream and talk, but nope — the best way to handle **Dadcrazy** was to lie down, close my eyes, and mumble, "Verge Aplo is the best singer in the world."

This was not that easy to do, because I very nearly revealed how I truly felt by making a completely icked-out face.

Dad screamed, **"YES!"** and ran out of the room to go do more crazy someplace else, which is pretty much always the point: **Move the Crazy Along.**

Hey! Maybe that's my thing. Maybe by my birthday, I can declare myself the youngest professional Dad Psychologist in the world, and people will bring their dads to me to cure them of **Dadcrazy.**

Some examples of DADCRAZY

Belief that meat is a vegetable.

Belief that clothes last forever and never need to be replaced.

Belief that meat is also a dessert and a medicine.

Sunday 22

Dear Dumb Diary,

Angeline called to **RSVP** to my party. I knew she'd come. People as pretty as Angeline are always looking for crowds to be pretty in. You rarely see pretty people **totally alone**. Their contrast to ugly people pleases them.

She asked me if I had bought any more Verge Aplo songs, and I told her that I already had them all and was just waiting for his new album to come out.

Then she asked if I thought he'd be good in concert, and I said **oh yeah totally oh my gosh are you serious he would totally rock your face off** and for sure I was going to see him in concert sometime this year. Then she asked if I thought his cane or bald head would interfere with my enjoyment. Or if the fact that he was dead would ruin it.

verge?

Dead.

Yeah.

Evidently, Mr. Aplo passed away some years ago and nobody was polite enough to stop playing his songs as though he was still alive.

Before I could scramble to come up with an **Incredibly Brilliant Excuse**, Angeline asked how I thought Jared Jay Fire would be in concert. I said he would be great unless he's dead, because I was paranoid she was doing it again.

Angeline laughed. "Jared's not dead," she said. "So it's not really Verge you like. And it's not Jared, either." She paused. "**Hmmmm**. Well, see you tomorrow."

VERGE
APLO

OK MY
MUSIC WAS
PRETTY BAD

You see? Angeline wants to copy me sooooo bad that she's not willing to just copy what I say or do. She's trying to pry open my head and see inside. She wants to copy me **deep, deep down.**

This makes me wonder if maybe she's not even really pretty. Maybe she's ugly and she's just copying pretty off somebody else.

How Angeline Did It?

1. SAW PRETTY GIRL.

Angeline →

2. TOTALLY COPIED OFF HER.

3. LIVED THIS LIE FOREVER.

I think she's given me a few more ideas for some party games.

"whose Cake was SPAT UPON?"

"Pin the tail on the Donkey"

"Pretty Piñata"

"Pin the Donkey on the Blond Girl"

Monday 23

Dear Dumb Diary,

Today was the day we all turned in our music posters. Except that right at the beginning of class, I raised my hand and asked if I could have a little extra time, because I still wasn't totally finished. I had my poster inside a big garbage bag, hidden from **copying eyeballs**.

Miss Anderson nodded and said okay. I really love Miss Anderson because she's pretty lazy, and when teachers are lazy like that, they're just so darned lovable. They're like pears that are just perfectly ripe.

And will soon be **utterly worthless**.

new unripe teacher   perfect   retired teacher

So, of course, Angeline raised her hand to ask for more time, followed by Vicki, and Emmily, and Isabella.

Miss Anderson is used to this sort of thing and she just nodded, gave them until Thursday, and reached into her big bowl of mints that she never shares and we are pretty sure are giant aspirins.

So deep is their need to copy me that they **are actually going to wait until I turn in my poster to complete theirs.**

And so, to blow their minds, I turned it in right then and there.

"**Oh!**" I said. "Oh. I forgot. I don't need any more time. I'm ready right now." And I slid my very special poster of the Whisker Brothers out of the garbage bag I was hiding it in.

HO-HO! They all thought it was going to be that old dead fart, Verge Aplo! But no. But no. But no.

But no.

Angeline's eyes almost popped out of her skull, but she quickly recovered and said, "The Whisker Brothers? Oh my gosh. That is *such* a coincidence." She quickly flipped her poster facedown to hide her Verge Aplo artwork.

I laughed prettily.

"I'm doing **MINE** on the Whisker Brothers," Angeline went on. Then, just like I predicted, Vicki, Emmily, and Isabella all lied the exact same thing, flipping their Verge Aplo posters over as well.

"That's great!" I said in a voice so convincing that the **Awesome Acting Alarm** at the Academy Awards office probably went off.

"We're like one big, happy Whisker Brothers fan club," I said.

Quick! Get this Award to Jamie Kelly!

I asked Miss Anderson if I could help hang the posters in the hall, and she said she'd let me know when she was going to do it.

Hmmmm. Yes. This is going to be . . . **interesting**.

I know, I know, it's wrong for a girl to keep secrets from her diary, but you'll just have to trust me on this. What are you going to do about it anyway? Give me a paper cut?

Tuesday 24

Dear Dumb Diary,

Yep. As I predicted, the Whisker Brothers have taken over the school. News traveled fast that they were my favorite band, I guess, and their faces were quickly taped up inside locker doors from the computer lab all the way to that boys' bathroom that smells like an orangutan wedding.

Kids listening to iPods bobbed their heads to the partially awful songs, and Emmily already had another one of her custom T-shirts going.

All in all, I'd say it was a **Whisker Brothers Day.**

The very peculiar thing is that, when I got home, Mom seemed to know it, too. Dad had this big, insane **dadsmile** on his face, and asked me if I had listened to any radical new Whisker Brothers songs today.

And then he **named a couple songs**.

He asked, "Did you listen to '**Girl U R Cute as 4 Puppy Butts, but Not 5 Cause That Would Be Weird**' or maybe '**Your Acne Medicine Smells Like Moonlight**'?"

Just exactly **HOW** Dad knew Whisker Brothers songs is a mystery to me, but I think I speak for all young people everywhere when I say we have to limit parental access to radios.

Or maybe my parents have been into my diary??

Also, we should never let parents see people dance

Because it might give them the idea to dance.

Wednesday 25

Dear Dumb Diary,

I wonder if the Whisker Brothers would have been willing to endure those countless hours of music lessons and those grueling months on the road playing lousy gigs if they knew their smiling babyish faces would only wind up on Vicki Vonder's T-shirt.

Even Isabella had taped a picture of them on her binder. I had to ask her why.

"So," I said at lunch, "you're a **Whisker Brothers fan,** huh?"

"I don't know," she said, and went back to poking her finger through her sandwich. (She likes them better with **stab wounds.**)

Then Emmily sat down next to us and smiled. She had written "Whisker Brothers" on her hand.

I asked Emmily if she was a Whisker Brothers fan, and then repeated the question four times because she didn't know who I was talking about.

Angeline came and joined us, followed (as always) by a little crowd of fans.

She took a bite of her sandwich, which was probably a perfectly balanced meal made just for her by little **cupid-chefs in sammich heaven.**

"Whisker Brothers," she said, and she grinned. **And grinned.** And then her eyes grinned and her nostrils grinned and her ears grinned.

"yeah," I said. And I must have said it just that way, in small, lowercase letters, because all of a sudden, all seven of Angeline's grins faded.

Vicki and Emmily and Isabella all noticed that Angeline's grin faded immediately, because whenever Angeline stops smiling, it feels like you just walked out of the sunshine into the cold, damp shade.

Angeline took a bite of her crustless sandwich and chewed it slowly, eyeing me with her suspicious baby-blue eyes, which I felt cut into me like **really pretty laser beams.**

Lasers are unattractive and immature

Thursday 26

Dear Dumb Diary,

Miss Anderson asked if I could help hang our posters after school today. I even made arrangements for Aunt Carol to drive me home afterward.

I asked Emmily to help, too, because she's the only one I knew I could trust to be **perfectly stupid**. In this way — and only this way — she is extraordinarily reliable.

Miss Anderson didn't hang the posters very adorably because there were no men teachers or custodians in the hall. She let us use her **precious precious tape**, but only she could hold the dispenser. Like most teachers, Miss Anderson has certain objects that she treasures above all else and jealously guards from students. Her tape is the main one.

Each school has ONE PAIR of scissors that work.

TEACHERS WILL NOT ADMIT THIS oR LeT you use them.

After about forty minutes or so, we were done. Miss Anderson thanked us for helping and we said good-bye.

But before we left, I stopped in front of my poster for just a moment. I looked up at the glorious artwork I did of the Whisker Brothers, on the **thin, thin, thin** sheet of poster board.

Here comes the secret I've been keeping from you, DUMB DIARY...

That's right. It's *really* thin. It's so thin, in fact, that sometimes, you don't notice right away if you're holding one sheet or two. And if somebody — let's say a pretty and clever, young, brunette, middle-school someone like myself — were to carefully stick two sheets together with a few tiny dots of glue here and there, there's a very good chance that a permanently distracted art teacher might not even notice.

And **later**, if a pretty and clever, young, brunette, middle-school someone unstuck that second sheet of poster board from the first, she might be able to reveal . . .

pick
pick
pick

Can you stand the suspense?
(fabulous ring added for drama)

THAT'S RIGHT. HER SECRET BAND: FATAALD! BWAH-HA-HA-HA-HA-HA-HA-HA!!!!

This was not just an average poster, either. It was a fabulous, magnificent example of what you can do when you sincerely care about a band and also about making the people who copy you eat it. **If I do say so myself.**

Emmily stood and stared at it in awe for a minute. Then she said, sweetly and sincerely, "My foot itches."

I have no idea if that was a compliment or not, but let's just say it was.

We just assume they're all compliments

I'm sorry I had to keep this little part of my plan a secret from you, Dumb Diary, but I was afraid that Isabella was reading you again and would find out.

Isabella has learned **many secrets** of mine through diary stealing.

TOP SECRETS
ISABELLA HAS ALREADY LEARNED

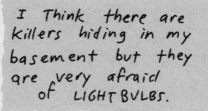
I Think there are killers hiding in my basement but they are very afraid of LIGHT BULBS.

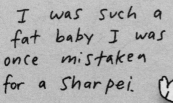
I ONCE FARTED SO HARD I MADE A MALL SANTA QUIT HIS JOB.

I was such a fat baby I was once mistaken for a Sharpei.

Dad brought home Chinese food for dinner, my favorite. I was in such a good mood that I hardly even became ill when he started singing along to a Whisker Brothers song on the radio.

I think they're all about to get taught a very important lesson about copying me. Especially Angeline.

They're just going to have to live with the fact that I'm just like them, **only better**.

Because I'm prettier...

And my Brain is smarter...

And my brain is prettier.

This evening, I'll be celebrating my victory against copycatting by crafting a playlist of music for my party. FATAALD will be the main feature, of course, possibly along with a few other bands that I think everybody will agree are quite good, but not as good as FATAALD.

I may include a Jared Jay Fire tune, but only so I can quickly run over and make a big spectacle of **shutting it off**. Maybe I'll do that with Verge Aplo, too. I don't know.

The only thing I know for sure is that we **won't** be listening to the Whisker Brothers.

everybody needs a MUSIC HAMMER!

Friday 27

Dear Dumb Diary,

Angeline stomped up to me at my locker today before school even started.

"What's with the poster?" she demanded.

"What are you talking about?" I said, stepping away from my locker door a bit so she could see all of the FATAALD stuff taped up inside.

"You were all into the Whisker Brothers," she said. Her immaculate nostrils flared, yet still seemed in perfect proportion.

"The Whisker Brothers? They're awful," I said.

"I KNOW THAT," Angeline yelped. I looked down at her notebook, which had a picture of the most repellant Whisker Brother of all taped to it.

She headed off in a **cloud of anger** that I found sort of refreshing, compared to her normal cloud of rainbows and helpful forest birds that usually follow her to attend to her ball gown and tiara and so forth.

Later, I noticed that many of the lockers that had been sporting pictures of the Whisker Brothers, Jared Jay Fire, or Verge Aplo were now empty. It was like an entire culture had been wiped out by a gigantic meteor and the survivors didn't know what to do instead. It just makes me feel that giant meteors are **more adorable** than I previously thought.

Hi! I'm here to destroy stuff! LOL!

Okay! But just the DUMB STUFF! LOL!

By lunchtime, Vicki wasn't even carrying her iPod, and she was wearing a hoodie over her shirt. You could just barely see the Whisker Brothers pathetically peeking out over the zipper pull, as if to say, **"Jamie. Please. Help us. Make us cool again."**

And I looked solemnly at the T-shirt and quietly answered, **"No."**

Mom was in a grouchy mood when I got home, and Dad didn't even show up until a few hours after dinner.

Stinker and Stinkette were hiding under things, probably because their dog senses picked up that the Whisker Brothers had been rejected so forcefully that somebody could be injured by their **falling popularity.**

Plus, whenever Mom is grouchy, we all kind of hide under things.

I'm not sure why Mom was grouchy, but since she is an adult, it's easy to narrow it down to one of two things:

1. Something she has every right to be grouchy about.

2. Something she has no right to be grouchy about.

Later on, Dad came up to my room to say good night.

"Big day tomorrow," he said.

"My birthday party!" I squealed.

"Your birthday party," he repeated. He was smiling, but he also sounded a bit FATAALD when he said it.

The Birthday Scream is so High-Pitched it can only be heard by Dogs and Parents

Saturday 28

Dear Dumb Diary,

TODAY WAS MY BIRTHDAY PARTY.

Isabella came, of course, and Emmily. Hudson Rivers was there representing cute boys, and Tucker was there representing boys who used to be ugly but have been transformed, somehow, into someone less ugly.

Margaret the pencil-chewer was there. That was comforting, because if the party was invaded by **giant pencil people**, she could handle them for us.

Mike Pinsetti came, too. I felt strange inviting him because I hate him, but somehow he seems to belong. He's like that piece of parsley on the plate at a restaurant that you don't want and would never actually eat, but it makes the plate seem more complete somehow. Maybe that was the destiny he was born to fill: **the World's Parsley Sprig.**

Anika came, and our friend Spitty Elizabeth, who we don't call Spitty Elizabeth to her face. Spitty Elizabeth was born with **buckets** where the rest of us have tiny saliva glands. You need to move quickly if you don't want to get doused when she talks.

I was shocked when Vicki walked in. Evidently, Isabella had filled out an invitation for her, back when she was helping me out with the party planning.

Since I had totally beaten everybody who was copying me with my **brilliant plan** to make them believe that I really liked the Whisker Brothers, I wasn't feeling as aggressive toward Vicki as I had before.

Also, I've noticed that being handed a gift tends to calm me down a little.

We ate pizza and ice cream and cake, and then everybody told me to start **opening presents**.

The first one was a Whisker Brothers CD. I smiled and said thanks and then opened another Whisker Brothers CD.

This was followed by a Whisker Brothers T-shirt and a Whisker Brothers bath towel.

I got Whisker Brothers pencils from Margaret, and a Whisker Brothers wastebasket from Emmily.

Even Isabella had gotten me a Whisker Brothers tote bag.

And I realized. **I had Whisker Brothered myself.** They all believed I liked the Whisker Brothers. I was looking at the largest collection of Whisker Brother merchandise I had ever seen. I owned it, and it was **all my fault**.

Isabella leaned in and whispered to me, "I don't even know why you like these guys so much. I think they stink."

"Wait a second," I whispered back. "You were listening to their music. You had their pictures up in your locker. If you hate them, why did you copy me like that?"

Isabella wolfed down her fifth piece of pizza. "I wasn't copying you. I was copying Emmily."

"**Emmily???????**" I said, adding additional **???????**s with the expression on my face.

Isabella explained that Emmily is the **happiest person** we've ever known. She thought if she just did what Emmily did, she would be happy — and Isabella is very curious about what happiness might feel like.

Emmily, hearing her name, wandered up. I asked her if she even really liked the Whisker Brothers, or if she was just copying me.

"**I was copying Vicki.** And it's really hard, too, because she changes so much." She smiled dumbly. "But I like her because she reminds me of that cartoon squirrel on that show I like with the cartoon squirrel."

Emmily said she hadn't really noticed what band I liked, but she supposed it was probably the Whisker Brothers because of all the Whisker Brothers stuff she suddenly noticed in front of us.

Actually, it wasn't a show. It was a commercial.

And it was a turtle. What can I say— I understand how Emmily misunderstands.

Angeline strolled over and smiled. I asked her why she kept copying all of my bands.

"I wasn't copying you," she said, and my mouth fell open wide enough to park a small, cute car in.

"Every single band you found out I liked, you copied," I said. "You know you did. You even pretended to like bands because you *thought* I liked them."

Angeline laughed.

"I didn't exactly *copy* them, Jamie. It was my **birthday present** to you. I wanted to help **your** favorite band become the trend. I thought you'd like to be the trendsetter."

"You know how you like to feel superior to everybody," Isabella gurgled through an esophagus full of pizza. (She's wrong about that, of course. I'm a much, much, **much** better person than that.)

"Well," I said, "you can't deny that Vicki's been copying my bands."

Angeline smiled and spoke quietly. "Vicki was copying **me**. She has been for a long time. Vicki's trying hard to fit in this year. She's making changes, and copying makes that easier. I don't mind. It's flattering, isn't it? Besides, nobody **owns** a band or a trend or a fashion."

Angeline picked up one of the Whisker Brothers CDs. "I know you don't really like this band, but don't you think we should play one of these?" she asked, adding in a whisper, "Aunt Carol and I know everybody at the mall. We can help you exchange the rest of the Whisker Brothers stuff for other things tomorrow."

NOT ME?

okay, that's just insulting

The rest of the party was a lot of fun.

We didn't need games, because Pinsetti and Tucker and Hudson did a lip synch to some of the Whisker Brothers songs, and we all screamed and pretended to like it. It was kind of weird. I wouldn't have liked it if they had done that with FATAALD. Oh, terrible bands of the world, perhaps your gift to us is your awfulness, so that we may **delight in mocking you.**

We all ate too much pizza and cake, and my parents had to yell at us six times to be quiet. That's a pretty good party. My last one only generated **three yells.**

How To Interpret Yell Count

 **ONE YELL** — Not a boring party, but probably nothing to remember.

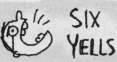 **SIX YELLS** — Awesome party. Injuries likely. Loads of fun.

 **TEN YELLS** — The police are on their way. Everybody get your stories straight.

Sunday 29

Dear Dumb Diary,

Today was my real birthday. When I came down to breakfast, Mom and Dad had set up a breakfast of donuts and ice cream, my favorite birthday breakfast. (And notice once more: circular foods = delicious.)

Dad slid an envelope across the table to me. "Happy birthday," he said.

I tore it open and peeked inside. **It was a ticket to a FATAALD concert.**

"How did you . . ." I started to ask.

"It wasn't easy, Jamie," he said. "Not easy at all. I had FATAALD tickets a long time ago, but I sold them and bought tickets to a Jared Jay Fire concert, instead. Then you were into Verge Aplo. Tickets to his concert were really hard to find because, as it turns out, he died. Did you know that?"

I nodded.

DONUT   ICE CREAM   MILKSHAKE (TOP VIEW)   BALL OF FUDGE

More proof that Roundness = Delicious

"Then," he continued, "it was these Whisker Brothers."

"And you bought Whisker Brothers tickets?" I asked.

"Nope," he said. "I almost did, but I listened to them instead. And to me, they sounded about as bouncy as your old pogo stick — **and just as useless**. Nope, for some reason, I thought that maybe you wouldn't stick with them. I bought FATAALD tickets again, instead."

My mom added that he'd had to go halfway across the state to pick them up in time for my birthday.

Dad went on, "But I have to admit, when I saw all the stuff you got yesterday, I was worried I had made a mistake. I asked your Aunt Carol if I should try to get the Whisker Brothers tickets after all."

"She asked Angeline, and Angeline told her I should hold on to these." Dad shrugged. "Good thing, too, because I had my car keys in my hand."

"Dad, you hate FATAALD," I said.

He admitted that it was true, but that he hates most of the things I like, **and that's okay**.

"I'm taking you, you know," he said. "You'll be okay with your dad being there at a concert, right?" He smiled. "I mean, I'll stay in the background. I'll make sure FATAALD doesn't even know I'm there."

"It'll be great," I said, thinking it would also be weird, but I'll make sure to **choose what he wears** so it won't be as bad.

NO

YES

"And one other thing," he said. "There was a hitch."

I knew it.

This was the part where I fall off the pogo stick and break my arm and get an ucky beagle. I braced myself.

I was pretty sure this was going to happen again

"There was a cancellation, and the ticket guy would only sell me these if I bought **six of them.**"

"Don't look at me. I'm not going," Mom added quickly.

"So figure out who you want to go with us," Dad said.

That wasn't hard to do.

Isabella is always there for me. Lots of times she's there to rob me, but she's always there.

Emmily, through her perfect dumbness, is teaching Isabella (and maybe me, too) to be sweeter.

Angeline started this problem for me, but she was doing it because she thought I'd like it. And maybe I did. Plus, in the end, she's the reason I finally wound up with these tickets, instead of tickets to see the Whisker Brothers.

Angeline, Emmily, and Isabella are **just like me, only better.** And so they're going with me.

And I think I know my accomplishment: **having awesome friends.** That's way better than playing a violin on a pogo stick when you're a little brat! Right?

Why Did I think

This might be COOL??

UGH. I sound like one of the awful shows the Whisker Brothers are on. Let's get real. It's not even close to playing a violin on a pogo stick when you're a little brat. Having awesome friends is not an accomplishment of *mine*, it's an accomplishment of *theirs*.

Oh, well. I have a year to come up with something before my next birthday, and I'm not going to let violin-playing pogo-stick girl bother me. On the bright side, she'll probably fall and scratch up her dad's car anyway.

Thanks for listening, Dumb Diary.

Jamie Kelly

Hey! Look!
Happy Birthday
to Me!

P.S. We took a vote, and we all decided that the last concert ticket should go to Vicki. Actually, Isabella didn't care who it went to, and Emmily voted for it going to Verge Aplo, but Angeline and I agreed. When I called Vicki, she might have actually cried, but who can blame her? **I'm letting her date my band!**

NEW DIARY.

NEW BEGINNING.

TAKE A PEEK AT JAMIE'S NEXT
TOP-SECRET DIARY....

DID YOU <u>REALLY</u> THINK
IT WOULD BE THAT EASY?

candy APPLE™

Read them all!

Life, Starring Me!

Callie for President

Drama Queen

I've Got a Secret

Confessions of a Bitter Secret Santa

Super Sweet 13

The Boy Next Door

The Sister Switch

Snowfall Surprise

Rumor Has It

The Sweetheart Deal

The Accidental Cheerleader

The Babysitting Wars

Star-Crossed

Accidentally
Fabulous

Accidentally
Famous

Accidentally
Fooled

Accidentally
Friends

How to Be a Girly Girl in
Just Ten Days

Ice Dreams

Juicy Gossip

Making Waves

Miss Popularity

Miss Popularity
Goes Camping

Miss Popularity
and the Best Friend Disaster

Totally Crushed

Wish You Were Here,
Liza

See You Soon,
Samantha

Miss You, Mina

Winner Takes All

CAN'T GET ENOUGH OF JAMIE KELLY?

CHECK OUT HER OTHER
DEAR DUMB DIARY
BOOKS!